SAN FRANCISCO

NL WEST

GIANTS

MICHAEL E. GOODMAN

Published by Creative Education, Inc.

123 S. Broad Street, Mankato, Minnesota 56001

Art Director, Rita Marshall
Cover and title page design by Virginia Evans
Cover and title page illustration by Rob Day
Type set by FinalCopy Electronic Publishing
Book design by Rita Marshall

Photos by Duomo, Focus on Sports, National
Baseball Library, Michael Ponzini, Bruce
Schwartzman, Spectra-Action, The Sporting News,
Sports Illustrated, UPI/Bettmann, Ron Vesley and
Wide World Photos

Library of Congress Cataloging-in-Publication Data

Goodman, Michael E.

  San Francisco Giants / by Michael E. Goodman.

  p. cm.

  Summary: A team history of the Giants, who
arrived in San Francisco in 1958 from Brooklyn
where they had played for seventy-five years,
thrilling fans on both coasts.

  ISBN 0-88682-453-2

  1. San Francisco Giants (Baseball team)—History—
Juvenile literature. [1. San Francisco Giants
(Baseball team)—History. 2. Baseball—History.]
I. Title.

GV875.S34G66 1991   91-10137

796.357'64'0979461—dc20   CIP

THE HOME OF THE GIANTS

No city in the United States is as famous for its beauty and excitement as San Francisco, California. San Francisco sits atop a series of steep hills, surrounded on three sides by water and connected to the rest of California by two well-known bridges—the Golden Gate and the San Francisco-Oakland Bay Bridge. Strong winds and thick fogs often sweep across these bridges and cover the city, giving it an air of mystery that adds to its dramatic beauty.

One of the places in which the winds blow strongest is San Francisco's Candlestick Park, where the San Francisco Giants have been playing baseball since 1960. That was two years after the club moved cross-country from its former home in New York City to the city by the Bay.

Hall of Famer Bill Terry.

The Giants brought to their new home in 1958 a long tradition of playing hard-nosed, winning baseball. San Francisco's baseball fans knew all about the great Giants stars of the past, such as Christy Mathewson, Frankie Frisch, Bill Terry, Mel Ott, Carl Hubbell, Bobby Thomson, and Sal Maglie. Soon they had their own new Giants heroes, including Willie Mays, Willie McCovey, Orlando Cepeda, Juan Marichal, and Bobby Bonds. The Giants of the 1990s are building a winning tradition, too, with new stars who promise to keep San Francisco on top of the baseball world for years to come.

Buck Ewing, who was later inducted into the Hall of Fame (1939), became a member of the Giants.

"MY BIG FELLOWS! MY GIANTS!"

The Giants began their National League history in New York City in 1883, seventy-five years before their move to San Francisco. The club wasn't called the Giants in those days, but was known as the New York Nationals. The Nationals played their home games in an open field just north of New York's Central Park that had been used for polo matches and, as a result, was referred to as the Polo Grounds. (The same name was later given to a new Giants' stadium built a little farther uptown.)

The Nationals were among the top teams in the league. They were led on both offense and defense by Buck Ewing, the best hitting and fielding catcher of his era and the first player in the nineteenth century to earn over five thousand dollars a year. New York fans loved to watch Ewing play, and he enjoyed showing off for them. During one game, he led off the top of the tenth inning with a single and proceeded to steal both second

Giants' star Kevin Mitchell.

and third base. Standing on third, Ewing turned to the crowd and shouted, "It's getting late. I'm going to steal home and we can then all have dinner." A few pitches later, everyone was heading home as Buck slid safely across home plate.

The Nationals' manager, James Mutrie, was particularly proud of Ewing and his other stars. As the players headed to or from the bench, he would cheer them on by shouting, "Come on, my big fellows, my giants!" A New York sportswriter heard Mutrie and started using the nickname in his stories. Soon everyone was calling the team the New York Giants.

The Giants won back-to-back National League pennants in 1888 and 1889, but then faded to the middle of the league standings until the beginning of the twentieth century. That was when a tough Irishman named John McGraw took control of the club and launched its "golden era."

"ONLY ONE MANAGER"

When twenty-eight-year-old John McGraw arrived in New York late in 1902, the Giants were at a low point. The team was in last place, far behind the league-leading Pittsburgh Pirates. Under McGraw's leadership, and behind the pitching of two amazing athletes—Joe McGinnity and Christy Mathewson—the club finished a solid second in the standings in 1903 and then first in both 1904 and 1905.

McGinnity was called "Iron Man" because he never seemed to get tired. Three times in August 1903 he hurled both games of doubleheaders and won all six contests. McGinnity's iron arm helped him record thirty-one wins in 1903 and thirty-five in 1904.

As good as McGinnity was, Mathewson was even better. From the beginning, "Matty" was McGraw's favorite. Horace Fogel, the Giants' manager before McGraw, had planned to make Mathewson the team's first baseman because of his size and fielding ability. Luckily for Giants fans, McGraw didn't agree. "That's the dumbest thing I ever heard of," McGraw bellowed when he arrived in New York. "Mathewson has the most natural pitching motion I've ever seen."

In perhaps his finest season, Christy Matthewson led all Giant pitchers with thirty-seven victories.

McGraw was right. Combining a rocket fastball and a sweeping curve with an unusual pitch called a "fadeaway" (known as a screwball today), Mathweson proceeded to mow down National League batters at a record pace for more than a dozen years. He finished his career with 372 victories and over twenty-five hundred strikeouts. "There never was any pitcher like Mathewson," McGraw said. "And I doubt there ever will be."

McGraw pushed players like McGinnity and Mathewson—and later New York stars such as Frankie Frisch, George Kelly, Casey Stengel, and Ross Youngs—and brought out the best in them. He was a real dictator on the field. "The main idea," he always said, "is to win." And that's what the Giants did. During McGraw's thirty-one years at the helm (1902–1932), the Giants captured ten pennants and had eleven second-place finishes.

During one amazing stretch in the early 1920s, the Giants won four straight National League titles. They also recorded back-to-back World Series triumphs over Babe Ruth's Yankees in 1921 and 1922, and came within one

A pitching great of today, Scott Garrelts.

Second baseman Robby Thompson.

In only his fourth full season Mel Ott (right) established a club record by driving in 151 runs.

out of winning a third championship against the Washington Senators in 1924.

Throughout his career, McGraw was both feared and respected by his players and his opponents. As the legendary Connie Mack once said, "There has been only one manager, and his name is John McGraw."

"MEMPHIS BILL," "MASTER MELVIN," AND "KING CARL"

Though McGraw didn't win any pennants in his last few seasons with the Giants, he did develop three players who would lead the team back to the top of the National League in the 1930s—Bill Terry, Mel Ott, and Carl Hubbell.

Terry, a lanky first baseman from Memphis, Tennessee, was a remarkable hitter. He had a lifetime batting average of .341, and was the last National League batter to hit over .400 in a season. Terry was also the best fielding first baseman of his era. Then, in 1932, he took on a new responsibility when McGraw asked him to become the team's manager.

The new player-manager took over a team that had finished in sixth place in 1932, but he was certain the club would bounce back. "We'll do third or better," he told writers. Why was Terry so confident? He knew he had two of the best hitters in the league, Mel Ott and himself, and the best pitcher in "King Carl" Hubbell.

Ott had first joined the Giants in 1926 when he was only sixteen years old, so some writers called him "Master Melvin." He had one of the strangest batting styles of all time: as a pitch came toward the plate, Ott lifted his right foot—almost as if he were cocking a gun—and then shifted his weight forward and snapped his bat at the ball.

Some of the Giants' coaches wanted to change Ott's style, but McGraw wouldn't let them. "Do what's comfortable for you," McGraw told his young star. Once again McGraw proved right. He knew Ott's swing was perfect for the short right-field fence in the Polo Grounds. By the time Master Melvin retired in 1947, he had become only the third player in major league history to hit more than five hundred homers. (The other two were Babe Ruth and Jimmy Foxx.)

The third part of Bill Terry's winning plan in 1933 was lefty pitcher Carl Hubbell. Hubbell had the most unhittable screwball since Christy Mathewson. It tied National League batters in knots throughout the 1930s, as the pitcher went on to win 253 games, a total second

1 9 3 2

Besides directing the Giants to the NL championship Bill Terry also led the club with 225 hits.

only to that of Mathewson in Giants' history. Hubbelll also had terrific control. One time, in 1933, Hubbell pitched all eighteen innings of a crucial game against St. Louis. Not only did he win the game, 1–0, but he didn't walk a single batter and struck out twelve. To this date, there has never been a performance to match that one!

Hubbell, Ott, and Terry had such great seasons in 1933 that the Giants surpassed Terry's expectations, coming in first place. The team was practically unstoppable, defeating the Washington Senators in the 1933 World Series.

The trio of New York stars also led the Giants to National League titles in 1936 and 1937. Then age began to take its toll on the players, and the club sank to the middle of the league standings where it remained throughout the 1940s.

TWO MORE GIANT MOMENTS IN NEW YORK

As the the 1950s began, Giants fans were longing for another winner in the Polo Grounds. They got their wish in 1951 when the Giants staged one of the greatest comebacks in National League history. In early August, New York trailed the Brooklyn Dodgers by a huge thirteen-and-a-half-game margin. Then the Giants got hot, winning thirty-seven of their last forty-four contests. Slowly, New York crept up on its crosstown rival, and the two teams finished the season in a dead heat. They faced off in a special best-of-three-games playoff for the National League pennant.

New York won game one on a Bobby Thomson home run. Brooklyn tied the series with a 10–0 blowout in

Like Bobby Thomson, shortstop Jose Uribe is a great athlete.

The talented Willie Mays joined the Giants and earned Rookie of the Year honors for his fine play.

game two. In the third and final contest, Brooklyn held a 4–1 lead in the bottom of the ninth inning. Giants fans were worried, but they got some encouragement when New York rallied for one run and had base runners on both second and third with one out. Up stepped Bobby Thomson, the hero of the first playoff game. Dodger manager Charlie Dressen brought in his best relief pitcher, Ralph Branca, to face Thomson. Branca tried to slip a high, inside fastball past the Giant batter, but the righty slugger stepped back from the plate as he swung and sent the ball sailing over the left-field stands for a three-run homer. As Thomson circled the bases, New York's radio announcer Russ Hodges began chanting, "The Giants win the pennant! The Giants win the pennant! They're going crazy! Ooooh, boy!" Giants fans will always remember that home run. They called it "The Miracle of Coogan's Bluff" (the place where the Polo Grounds was located).

A second miracle occurred in Coogan's Bluff just three years later, after New York had won another National League pennant. The Giants were taking on the favored Cleveland Indians in game one of the 1954 World Series. This time the hero was New York's superstar center fielder Willie Mays. With the score tied 2–2 in the top of the eighth inning and two Indian runners on base, Cleveland slugger Vic Wertz sent a line drive to the deepest part of center field in the Polo Grounds. Everyone was sure the shot would sail way over Mays's head and win the game for Cleveland. But Mays turned his to home plate and raced to where he thought the ball would come down. He judged the catch perfectly and grabbed the ball over his shoulder on the dead run. Then

Willie Mays and the famous catch.

Memories of Mays, first baseman Will Clark

The great Willie Mays (right) won his first of two National League MVP awards.

he whirled around and threw a strike back to the infield to hold the runners in place. Cleveland never recovered from that play. The Giants rallied to win game one in extra innings and then swept the next three contests from the brokenhearted Indians.

Mays's catch was amazing, but Giants fans in New York and later in San Francisco grew used to Willie's miracles in the field and at bat. Many baseball experts consider him to have been the greatest all-around player in baseball history. Said Leo Durocher, his long-time manager, "If somebody came up and hit .450, stole a hundred bases, and performed a miracle on the field every day, I'd look you in the eye and say that Willie was better. He could do the five things you have to do to be a superstar: hit, hit with power, run, throw, and field. And he had another magic ingredient...."

He lit up the room when he came in. He was a joy to be around."

Unfortunately for New York fans, they only got to watch Mays perform regularly for a few years, from 1951 to 1957. By the start of the 1958 season, Mays and the rest of the Giants had moved to their new home in San Francisco.

MAYS, MCCOVEY, AND MARICHAL SHINE ON

When the Giants first arrived in San Francisco, local fans knew few of the players except Willie Mays, but they turned out in record numbers to cheer for their new heroes. Mays had no trouble adjusting to the sun and winds of northern California. In his first year on the West Coast, the multitalented Mays batted .347, hit twenty-nine homers, drove in ninety-six runs, and led the league in runs scored (121) and stolen bases (thirty-one). Yet, in the fans' voting for Most Valuable Giant in 1958, Mays came in second to rookie sensation Orlando Cepeda. San Francisco fans always had a special feeling for Cepeda, because he was the first Giants star who began his career in the city by the Bay.

The next year, the local fans had another "home-grown" hero to cheer—Willie "Stretch" McCovey. San Franciscans knew McCovey would be someone special from the first night he put on a Giants uniform. The 6'4" slugger tripled his first time at bat and finished the game with two triples and two singles. Even though he played only fifty-two games in 1959, he was easily elected National League Rookie of the Year. When veteran pitcher Lew Burdette of the Braves was asked which

Under the direction of manager Bill Rigney the Giants finished their first season in San Francisco in third place.

Willie McCovey.

pitch McCovey could hit best, he replied, "He hits curves, sliders, and fastballs—everything I can throw at him."

Mays, Cepeda, and McCovey were soon joined in San Francisco by a young hurler from the Dominican Republic named Juan Marichal. Marichal had three things a great pitcher needs—speed, control, and confidence. He put all three to work the first time he took the mound in 1960. Facing the Philadelphia Phillies, Marichal had a no-hitter going until catcher Clay Dalrymple singled with two outs in the eighth inning for the Philadelphia's only hit.

Afterwards, writers swarmed around the young pitcher, who could speak only a few words of English. Cepeda served as translator. A reporter asked, "Were you surprised at how well you performed today?"

"He says, 'No,'" Cepeda reported. "'I expected to win. I always expect to win.'" By the time he finished his Hall of Fame career, Marichal had registered 243 wins and nearly twenty-three hundred strikeouts.

With their talent and confidence, the Giants returned to the top of the National League. San Francisco won pennants in both 1962 and 1971, and came close to bringing a world championship to their new home in 1962. The Giants battled the Yankees evenly in the 1962 World Series, and trailed by one run going into the bottom of the ninth inning of game seven. Then the Giants got two runners on base, with Willie McCovey coming to bat. As San Francisco fans stood and screamed, "Stretch" hit a scorcher right at Yankee second baseman Bobby Richardson. If the ball had been just a few inches to the right or left, the Giants

1 9 6 6

For the fourth consecutive season Juan Marichal recorded over twenty victories, with twenty-five wins.

Left to right: Bobby Bonds, Dave Kingman, John Montefusco, Juan Marichal.

would have won the game and the series. But it was not to be.

The Giants began a decline in the early 1970s. Aging stars Mays and McCovey were traded and Marichal was released, and although young players like Bobby Bonds, Dave Kingman, Gary Matthews, Jack Clark, and John "the Count" Montefusco arrived to take their places, they just didn't have the talent to keep the team on top.

John ("The Count") Montefusco struck out 215 batters on his way to winning Rookie of the Year honors.

THE GREAT TURNAROUND

When the Giants started losing regularly in the late 1970s and early 1980s, fewer fans came to the games at Candlestick Park. Team owner Bob Lurie threatened to sell the franchise or to move it to a different city. Luries threats upset both the fans and players in San Francisco, who pinned their hopes of keeping the team on the Giants' new manager, Roger Craig, and new general manager, Al Rosen, who took charge of the club in 1986. These two men led the team in a great turnaround. "We're going to get back to the basics," Craig announced. "If we can discipline ourselves to do the little things right, the big things will take care of themselves."

Rosen also got into the act, promoting three young infielders—Will Clark, Robby Thompson, and Jose Uribe—to the Giants' squad, and trading for outfielder Candy Maldanado. Clark earned his nickname, "The Thrill", right away. He homered in his first time at bat in the majors, against Houston in the Astrodome, and hit another home run in his first game in Candlestick a week later. The Giants and their young star were on their way.

The Giants' home, Candlestick Park (pages 26–27). 25

By the time the 1986 season ended, San Francisco had won eighty-three games (twenty-one more than in 1985) and had jumped from last place to third in the NL West. Nearly seven hundred thousand more fans attended home games than during the previous year. For the time being, there was no more talk of moving the franchise.

"It's nice to win some games, but the Giants won't rest until we win the big one," said manager Craig. That was the Giants' goal in 1987, and they came close to reaching it, capturing their first NL West title since 1971. Then they took the St. Louis Cardinals to a seventh game in the National League Championship Series (NLCS) before losing the battle for the National League pennant and a shot at the World Series.

Two years later, however, San Francisco was back. Behind Will Clark and his new teammate Kevin Mitchell, the league's Most Valuable Player in 1989, the Giants swept to another NL West title. This time, they pounded the Chicago Cubs in the NLCS and faced off against the Oakland A's, the team from across the Bay, for the world championship.

Everyone expected an exciting World Series, but no one could have predicted the dramatic events that took place in October 1989. After Oakland won the first two games in its home park, the series moved to Candlestick. Half an hour before game three was to begin, a devastating earthquake shook the Bay Area. Baseball became a secondary concern that night, as players and fans huddled together in the stadium and said prayers of thanks because they were alive. Ten days later the series resumed, and Oakland completed a four-

Kevin Mitchell (left) was congratulated after slamming a two run homer against the Dodgers.

game sweep of the Giants. San Francisco fans were disappointed, but they were optimistic about the future.

A NEW DECADE

G iants supporters have good reason to be hopeful in the 1990s. For one thing, the club has Will "the Thrill" Clark, with his unmatchable combination of batting skill, power, and fielding excellence. "He has that look of a once-in-a-lifetime player—the Ted Williams, Mickey Mantle, Willie Mays kind of personality and performance that people just dream about," noted sportswriter Maury Allen.

But Clark will not be expected to do everything on his own. With Kevin Mitchell hitting behind Clark in the line-up, the Giants have the best back-to-back sluggers in the

Pitcher Atlee Hammaker.

Slugger Matt Williams.

1 9 9 1

Boosted by the performances of Will Clark and Dave Righetti the Giants were a powerful team.

majors. They also get additional offensive support from third baseman Matt Williams, who hit thirty-three homers and drove in 119 runs in 1990. "Before Williams joined the club, we just had a great one-two punch; now we have a great one-two-three," said teammate Robby Thompson.

Thompson provides important contributions of his own both on offense, with his speed and slashing hits, and on defense with his play at second base. "The Giants double-play combination of Thompson and Jose Uribe ranks as the NL best," commented baseball expert Eliot Cohen.

The team's only shortcoming may be its pitching; injuries have hurt the staff in recent years. But Roger Craig is certain that starters Scott Garrelts, Kelly Downs, and John Burkett, and relievers Jeff Brantley and Dave Righetti can get the job done and carry the team to the top.

It has been a long for the Giants from Coogan's Bluff to Candlestick Park. The team has thrilled fans on both the East Coast and the West Coast during its exciting history, and its winning tradition is likely continue in the new decade.